Witch, Goblin, and Ghost Are Back

Five I AM READING *Stories*
by Sue Alexander
pictures by Jeanette Winter

PANTHEON BOOKS

This book is dedicated with love
to Marilyn Marlow,
who believes in me even when
I don't believe in myself.

Text copyright © 1985 by Sue Alexander
Illustrations copyright © 1985 by Jeanette Winter
All rights reserved under International and Pan-American Copy-
right Conventions. Published in the United States by Pantheon
Books, a division of Random House, Inc., New York, and simul-
taneously in Canada by Random House of Canada Limited, Toronto.
Manufactured in the United States of America
1   3   5   7   9   10   8   6   4   2

Library of Congress Cataloging in Publication Data
Alexander, Sue, 1933–
Witch, Goblin, and Ghost Are Back.
(I am reading book)
Contents: The winter day—The painting—Goblin's fudge—
[etc.] [1. Friendship—Fiction] I. Winter, Jeanette, ill.
II. Title. III. Series.
PZ7.A3784Ar 1984 [E] 83-22157
ISBN 0-394-86296-1 ISBN 0-394-96296-6 (lib. bdg.)

THE STORIES

THE WINTER DAY

It was winter.

The pond in the meadow

was frozen over.

So Witch, Goblin, and Ghost

went ice-skating.

Witch skated figure eights.

Ghost skated big circles.

Goblin skated a slow, wobbly line.

w "This is fun!" Witch said.

"I do like to ice-skate."

gh "So do I," said Ghost.

Goblin didn't say anything.

gob "I don't really like to ice-skate,"

he thought.

"It makes my ankles hurt."

Then he thought,

"I should like it.

Witch and Ghost both do."

Goblin sighed.

Witch skated some more figure eights.

Ghost skated some more circles.

Goblin sat on a tree stump

and watched.

Then it started to snow.

"Let's go to my house," Witch said.

"I'll make dinner for us all."

"Oh, good!" said Goblin.

"That will be nice," said Ghost.

So off they went.

On the way to Witch's house,

Ghost said, "I like it

when the snow falls on my nose.

It tickles."

"It does tickle," Witch agreed.

"I like it too."

Goblin didn't say anything.

8

"I don't like it

when the snow falls on my nose,"

he thought.

"It makes me cold."

Then he thought,

"I should like it.

Witch and Ghost do.

Friends are supposed to like

the same things."

Goblin turned a sad shade of blue.

Witch made roast chicken for dinner.

She made mashed potatoes.

She made buttered broccoli, too.

"Oh my!" said Ghost.

"Broccoli is my favorite vegetable."

"I like it too," said Witch.

Goblin looked at Witch.

He looked at Ghost.

And then he began to cry.

w "Why, Goblin, what's the matter?"
asked Witch.

gh "Did you burn your tongue?"
asked Ghost.

gob "No," sobbed Goblin.
"But friends are supposed to like
all the same things.

"And I don't really like to ice-skate.
It makes my ankles hurt.

And I don't like snow
to fall on my nose.
It makes me cold.

And I don't like broccoli.
I don't like it at all!"

Witch didn't say anything.

She just looked at Goblin.

Ghost looked at Goblin too.

gh Then he said, "Goblin,

would you like to hear a story?"

Goblin sniffled. *SNIFFED* *101*

gok "Yes, Ghost, I would,"

he said. *24$*

He wiped his eyes.

"Once there was a goblin,"

said Ghost,

"who had two good friends.

They both liked

to ice-skate.

They both liked snow

to fall on their noses.

And they both

liked broccoli.

"Now, the goblin didn't like

any of those things.

But the goblin's friends

didn't care.

They knew that friends

don't need to like

all the same things.

They just need to like each other.

The end."

Witch clapped her hands.

"I like that story, Ghost,"

she said.

Goblin thought for a minute.

Then he said,

"I like that story too, Ghost.

I like it a lot."

"I'm glad," said Ghost.

Then he took another helping of broccoli.

So did Witch.

And Goblin took another helping

of mashed potatoes.

THE PAINTING

Witch was on her porch.

She was painting.

Goblin came up the path.

He looked at the picture

that Witch was painting.

"That's a nice painting, Witch!"

Goblin said.

"I love pictures of waterfalls."

Witch smiled.

"I know you do, Goblin," she said.

"That's why I'm painting one.

This picture will be for you."

Goblin turned a pleased shade of pink.

"Oh, how nice! Thank you, Witch,"

he said.

"Is it almost finished?"

"No," said Witch.

Goblin sat down on the porch.

He watched Witch paint.

gob "Why are you using so many colors,

Witch?" he asked.

W "Because there are lots of colors

in water," Witch said.

"Water takes on the colors

of everything around it.

It takes on the colors of the rocks,

the trees, and even the clouds

in the sky."

gob "Oh," said Goblin.

"I never thought of that."

"Do be quiet, Goblin," said Witch.

"It's hard to paint and talk

at the same time."

Goblin sat quietly

and watched Witch paint.

After a while he asked,

"Is the picture almost finished now?"

"No," said Witch.

Goblin sighed.

20

Then he stood up.

gob "I think I'll go for a walk,"

he said.

"Maybe when I get back,

the picture will be finished."

Witch didn't say anything.

She went on painting.

So off Goblin went.

He walked over the rocks
at the foot of the hills.

He walked through
the wildflowers
in the meadow.

He walked along the stream
in the Haunted Woods.
He walked for a very long time.

When he got back to Witch's house,

she was still painting.

"Isn't the picture finished *yet*, Witch?"

he asked.

"No," said Witch. "Not yet."

Goblin sighed.

"It's taking a long time, Witch,"

he said.

"And waiting is hard."

Witch didn't say anything.

She just went on painting.

Goblin walked back and forth.

Then he walked back and forth

some more.

He walked up the porch steps.

Then he walked down them.

"Do sit down, Goblin," said Witch.

"It's hard to paint

while you are moving all around."

"But Witch!" Goblin shouted.

"It's taking such a long time!

And waiting is very, very hard!"

Witch didn't say anything.

She just looked at Goblin.

He turned an embarrassed shade

of rose.

Then he sat down.

He sat as still as he could.

Witch went on painting.

After a long while Witch said,

"There! It's finished."

Goblin looked at the picture

Witch had painted.

He looked and he looked and he looked.

Then he said,

gob "It took a very long time, Witch.

And waiting was very, very hard.

But you know what?"

W "What?" asked Witch.

gob "It doesn't matter," Goblin said,

"when what you're waiting for

is as wonderful as this picture!"

And Goblin gave Witch a big hug.

GOBLIN'S FUDGE

Witch, Goblin, and Ghost

were on Witch's porch.

"I'm glad you decided

to make fudge today, Witch,"

said Goblin.

"It's my favorite snack.

I just love it."

He took another piece.

gh "It *is* delicious, Witch,"

said Ghost.

He took another piece too.

gob "I love fudge so much

that I could eat it

for breakfast, lunch, and dinner,"

Goblin said.

Ghost shook his head.

gh "I couldn't eat that much fudge,"

he said.

gob "*I* could," said Goblin.

"I don't think it would be
a good idea, Goblin,"
said Witch.

"Well, I *do*," Goblin said.
He turned a stubborn shade
of purple.

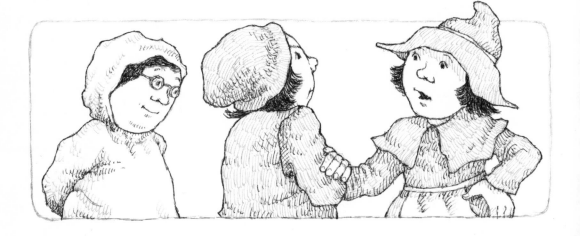

Later, when Goblin went home,
he thought about eating fudge.
He thought about eating it
for breakfast, lunch, and dinner.

"I'll do it!" he said.

So he made a big pan of fudge.

"Hmmm. My fudge isn't as good

as the fudge that Witch makes,"

Goblin said, licking the spoon.

"But it will do."

He put the fudge aside to cool.

Then he went to bed.

Goblin woke up early the next morning.

"Hooray!" he yelled.

"Today is going to be

a *delicious* day!"

He jumped out of bed

and ran into the kitchen.

Goblin ate six pieces of fudge

for breakfast.

"My, that was good," he said.

A little later
his stomach began to rumble. FX ?
"Hmmm," Goblin said.
"Maybe I didn't eat enough
for breakfast."
So he ate two more pieces of fudge.
Then he went outside to pull weeds
out of his garden.
While he was pulling weeds,
his stomach rumbled again.

"It must be time for lunch,"

Goblin said.

So he went inside

and ate twelve pieces of fudge.

"That was delicious!"

Goblin said when he was through.

A little later Goblin's stomach

began to feel a bit queer.

"Hmmm," he said.

"Maybe a long walk will stop my stomach

from feeling so queer."

So he went for a long walk.

While he was walking,

his stomach rumbled again.   *FX ?*

It rumbled louder

than it had before.

"I'd better have an early dinner,"

Goblin said.

So he went home

and ate the last fourteen pieces of fudge.

Then he took a book

and curled up in his chair to read.

While he was reading,

his stomach rumbled some more.

It felt very, very queer.

"Ohhhhhhh!" Goblin moaned.

"I don't feel very well.

I don't feel very well at all.

My stomach *hurts*!"

He turned a sick shade of green.

Just then he heard Witch's voice.

"Goblin," she called, "are you home?"

gob. "Ohhhhhhh!" moaned Goblin.

"Come in, Witch. Ohhhhhhh!"

Ghost came in with Witch.

W. "Whatever is the matter, Goblin?"

asked Witch.

gh. "Why are you moaning?"

"You look *sick*, Goblin," said Ghost.

gob "Ohhhhhh!" moaned Goblin.

"My stomach hurts.

It hurts a lot. Ohhhhhhh!"

"Goblin," asked Witch,

"did you eat fudge

for breakfast, lunch, and dinner?"

Goblin nodded.

"Oh dear," said Witch.

She hurried into the kitchen.

So did Ghost.

"Here, Goblin," Witch said.

"This should help."

She brought him a cup of tea
and some toast.

"This will help, too,"
said Ghost.
He brought Goblin
a hot-water bottle.

"Ohhhhhh!" moaned Goblin.
He ate the toast
and drank the tea.

Then he lay down on the sofa

and put the hot-water bottle

on his stomach.

"Ohhhhhhh!" he moaned again.

Witch and Ghost sat down.

They waited for Goblin

to feel better.

They waited and waited and waited.

After a long while Goblin sat up.

"I feel much better now,"

he said.

"Good," said Witch and Ghost.

Goblin thought for a minute.

Then he said,

"You know what, Witch?

You know what, Ghost?

Fudge is a very good *snack*."

And Witch and Ghost agreed.

THE MEADOW DAY

One day Ghost came to visit Goblin.

"Hello, Goblin," said Ghost.

"What are you doing?"

"Nothing!" said Goblin.

He walked back and forth.

Ghost watched him.

Then Ghost said,

"What's the matter, Goblin?"

"I don't know, Ghost,"

said Goblin.

"But I feel jumpy and out-of-sorts.

I have felt this way all day!"

And he walked back and forth

some more.

"Hmmm," said Ghost.

"It sounds to me as if you need

a meadow day."

Goblin stopped.

"What's that?" he asked.

"Come along and I'll show you,"

Ghost said.

"All right," said Goblin.

And off they went.

Soon they reached the meadow.

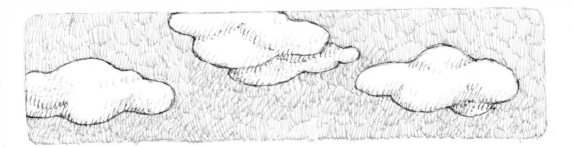

"Well, we're here," said Goblin.

"What do we do now?"

"Watch," said Ghost.

"Watch what?" asked Goblin.

"The clouds," said Ghost.

He lay down on the grass

and looked up at the sky.

Goblin shrugged.

Then he lay down on the grass

and looked up at the sky too.

Goblin saw long thin clouds.

He saw round puffy clouds.

"Look at that cloud, Ghost!" he said.

"It looks just like an elephant

with a long trunk!"

"So it does," Ghost agreed.

They both laughed.

Then they watched

more clouds drift by.

After a while Ghost sat up.

"What are you going to do now?"

Goblin asked.

"Listen," said Ghost.

"Listen to what?" Goblin asked.

"The wind," said Ghost.

"Oh!" said Goblin.

He sat up too.

Goblin heard the wind

whispering through the grass.

He heard it sighing
through the leaves on the trees.

He heard it whistling
around the rocks.

Goblin laughed.

gob "The wind has lots of voices,"
he said.

gh "So it does," Ghost agreed.
They both listened to the wind
some more.

Then Ghost said,

"Take some deep breaths, Goblin.

Breathe in the meadow smells."

Goblin did.

He breathed in the sweet smell

of fresh earth.

He breathed in the spicy smell

of wildflowers.

He breathed in the dusty smell

of tree bark.

gob "Oh my, Ghost," said Goblin.

"There are lots of different smells

in the meadow!"

gh "So there are," Ghost agreed.

Goblin and Ghost watched

some more clouds.

They listened to the wind some more.

They breathed in more meadow smells.

After a while Ghost said,

gh "Do you feel better now, Goblin?"

gob "Oh yes!" Goblin said.

gh "I thought you would," said Ghost.

Later, Ghost and Goblin

went back to Goblin's cave.

On the way Goblin said,

gob "You know what, Ghost?

Now that I know about meadow days,

I'm going to have more of them."

And he did.

GOBLIN'S RAFT TRIP

One afternoon Goblin got on his raft.

"Goodbye, Witch!" he said.

"Goodbye, Ghost!

I'll see you when I get back."

"Goodbye, Goblin," said Witch and Ghost.

"Have a good time!"

Goblin pushed his raft

away from the bank.

gob "This will be fun!" he said.

"Maybe I will go

all the way to the river.

Maybe I will even go

all the way to the *ocean*!"

He held on tight

to the steering pole.

And the raft floated slowly
down the stream.
Goblin steered the raft
past an old rotted log.

He steered it around
some big rocks.

He steered it through
a patch of water lilies.

A ribbon of fish swam by.

Goblin lay on his stomach to watch them.

Then he sat up to watch

a wedge of ducks.

And then he lay on his back

to look at the clouds.

While he was looking at the clouds

Goblin said, "I wonder what Witch

and Ghost are doing?"

Then he said,

"Maybe Ghost has made up a new story

and is telling it to Witch.

And maybe Witch has made

a pan of fudge

and is giving it to Ghost."

Goblin sighed.

After a while Goblin sat up

and looked around.

The stream was still going through

the Haunted Woods.

"Oh my," Goblin said.

"It's taking a long time

to get to the river.

It may take a *very* long time

to get to the ocean."

He dangled his feet in the water
and wiggled his toes.

"Hmmm," he said.

"If I am gone for a long time,

Ghost may forget

that I like to hear his stories.

And Witch may forget

that I like to eat her fudge."

Goblin pulled his feet

out of the water.

"Oh no!" he shouted.

"If I am gone for a *very* long time,

Witch and Ghost may forget ME!"

Goblin jumped up.

He took hold of the steering pole

and steered the raft back

the other way.

He steered it back through
the patch of water lilies.

He steered it back
around the big rocks.

He steered it back
past the old rotted log.

Goblin steered his raft

all the way back

to where he had started from.

He pushed his raft onto the bank.

And he ran all the way

to Witch's house.

"Witch!" Goblin called.

"I'm back! It's me, Goblin!"

Witch opened the door.

Ghost was right behind her.

"I know it's you, Goblin," said Witch.

"Ghost and I were wondering

when you'd be back."

Goblin sighed.

"Then you didn't forget me," he said.

"Of course not!" said Ghost.

"Even if you were gone

for a very long time,

we wouldn't *forget* you."

"No," said Witch.

"We would just miss you very much."

Goblin turned a happy shade of pink.

Then he told Witch and Ghost

all about his raft trip.

SUE ALEXANDER is the author of many outstanding books and stories for children and is on the board of directors of the Society of Children's Book Writers. She is the recipient of the 1980 Dorothy C. McKenzie Award, and her evocative book *Nadia the Willful* won the 1984 Distinguished Work of Fiction Award, both given by the Southern California Council on Literature for Children. She lives with her husband in Canoga Park, California.

JEANETTE WINTER's delightful illustrations animate all five Witch, Goblin, and Ghost story collections. Her recent books, *The Girl and the Moon Man* (a haunting Siberian folktale) and *Hush Little Baby*, are noteworthy additions to her growing body of work. She lives with her husband in Dallas, Texas.